MAGICAL PONY TALES

CHRISTINE
PULLEIN-THOMPSON

CAVALIER PAPERBACKS

Copyright © Christine Pullein-Thompson 1998

Illustrations copyright © Mark Smallman 1998

Published by Cavalier Paperbacks 1998
Burnham House
Jarvis St
Upavon
Wilts SN9 6DU

ISBN 1-899470-15-8

Printed and bound in Great Britain by Cox &
Wyman, Reading, Berks

CONTENTS

Annie's Amazing Ride   5

Flyaway and the Fantastic Pond   20

Minnie and the Miraculous   32
Mushrooms

Carlotta's Dream   48

Snowdrop and the Magic Bird   66

magical that Annie would never forget it. She was lying in a field full of wild flowers and lush green grass while Crispin her favourite pony at the riding school was blowing fresh pony-scented air into her face. "Wake up. We're going to fly," he said.

"But we haven't got wings," replied Annie, but when she looked at Crispin properly she saw that he had grown beautiful feathered wings.

Crispin knelt down in front of her. "Jump on," he said.

"Where are we going?" asked Annie nervously.

"To the end of the universe," said Crispin.

"I don't ride very well," replied Annie.

"Just hold on to my wings and you'll be all right," said Crispin.

His back was warm and there was just room for Annie to sit behind his wings, which started at his withers and spread out sideways.

"Hold tight," said Crispin. "I'm about to take off."

"How come you speak such good English?" asked Annie holding on as tight as she could to Crispin's flaxen mane.

"I learn it in my sleep," replied Crispin with a pony chuckle.

"What about my Mum and Dad and Josh, can they see me flying?" asked Annie, "because I don't want them to worry about me."

"They're all right," answered Crispin rising higher and higher into the air. "Stop worrying, let go of life, forget about maths and reading. Relax."

They were in the clouds now which were damp and frothy, but not cold.

"Look down and you will see London," said Crispin.

Birds flew past them. A grey haze rose above London. "That's smog," said Crispin. "London smog."

Soon after that, far below, Annie could

see the sea and ships bobbing on it like tiny toys. I feel quite safe, she thought. I can ride. If only Mum and Dad and Josh could see me now. I'm so high up, but I'm not scared at all.

Crispin had stopped flapping his wings. "We've picked up a current of air, we're going very fast now, faster than you've ever been before," he said.

"Where are we going?" asked Annie.

"I've told you once – to the end of the universe," said Crispin.

"And after that?" asked Annie.

"I don't know. But stop worrying. We're far away from everything. There's no riding lessons here, no school, no nasty bullies or spite, or envy. Only joy," said Crispin, relaxed and cruising on the warm current of air. "No nasty bits in our mouths, no chains, no heavy saddles, no metal shoes – we're free, Annie. We can be ourselves."

Annie did not answer, because she was thinking, no one can ever call me stupid or a coward again. And Jilly at the riding school won't be able to say, "Annie, you flap your arms and legs like a windmill when you ride" - not after this.

There were twinkling lights far below them now.

"We're over France," Crispin said.

"Are we going to eat anything. All this flying is making me hungry," said Annie.

"Not now, later," said Crispin.

"What's the time?" asked Annie next.

"Up here time doesn't exist," replied Crispin grandly. "Worry, time, money, newspapers, TV – they are just flotsam and jetsam. They are not important."

Annie thought of her father who worked on a newspaper and said nothing.

"We're reaching the Alps. We'll land in a minute. Hold on to my wings," said Crispin. "And keep your heels down."

Soon Annie could see the tops of mountains covered with snow. Crispin flew between them down into a valley full of flowers. Then he slowed by flapping his long wings backwards and made a perfect landing.

"Now look under my wings and you will find something to eat. It may be a bit warm but I can't help that," said Crispin.

Under his wings Annie found sandwiches full of sorrel, sliced apple in cabbage leaves, blackberry cake and parsnip wine.

"It's delicious," she said munching blackberry cake.

"No sugar, no meat, no nasty things," said Crispin. "Drink the wine out of the cabbage leaves. I recommend it."

Annie felt a little fuzzy in the head after the wine, while in the distance she could hear the tinkling of cows' bells and the bleating of sheep.

She felt like lying down on the grass and sleeping. But Crispin said that they must get going or they would never reach the end of the universe by bedtime.

Annie thought of her pretty bedroom at home, full of the books she couldn't read, and the teddy bear that slept with her, and the picture of a tiger which gave her bad dreams. And she did not miss any of it, not the tiniest bit.

So they flew on. Over the Mediterranean, the Black Sea, Russia and over Alaska where Annie could see polar bears far below playing in the snow. Over the Arctic, past frozen ships and people dressed in furs, on and on they flew.

"Aren't you tired, Crispin?" asked Annie.

"No, I'm never tired, not when I'm flying like this. At the riding school, it's different, but not up here. Up here tiredness does not exist," said Crispin. "Up here you live for ever."

And then at last Crispin landed again. "Here we are at the end of the universe.

Do you want to go home or go on for ever and ever?" he asked.

In front of Annie lay a path, wider than any path she had ever seen before. It was a mixture of gold and silver with a red sunset in the distance. It was so beautiful that it brought tears to Annie's eyes.

"It never ends," said Crispin, lying on the ground and stretching his wings. "You can stay here, or go back. If you go on along the path, you must go on alone, because only humans can go. Ponies are not allowed!"

"But that's not fair," cried Annie.

"So you must choose Annie. I'm going to sleep for a little while and when I wake I want your answer." And Crispin shut his eyes and fell into a deep sleep, gently snoring from time to time.

Annie sat on the sandy soil and thought and thought. She thought of her parents waiting for her at home, of her favourite teacher, Miss Coe missing her at school. She thought of Josh calling her to play dominoes. She thought of Mum crying and of Dad silent for days on end.

Then she looked at the silver and gold path which shimmered and sparkled and she thought, no more school, no more failure, no more nasty little girls sticking pins into me or stepping on my feet because I can't read.

Then she looked at Crispin who was so kind and sweet and good-natured but who could not go with her.

And so when at last he opened his eyes, she said, "I've made up my mind. I want to go back."

"Hop on then," said Crispin. "And we'll start straight away and we won't stop for anything, because tomorrow there's a gymkhana at the riding school and I'm expected to win the bending race."

They went a different way home. They flew over Canada and the USA and over the Atlantic Ocean, which was full of wild waves and Spain, Italy, and Switzerland. They passed aeroplanes full of tourists and thousands of migrating birds. Then they reached the smog again and Annie knew they were nearly home. She cried into Crispin's wings then, because now she didn't want the ride to end, she wanted to fly for ever and ever. Crispin said, "Your tears are washing my wings, Annie. Don't cry. You've chosen to return, so now you must put up with it. I shall be back in the riding school tomorrow and you will be with your mother and father. That is reality."

Afterwards Annie wasn't sure where they landed or whether they landed at all for the next thing she saw were her parents and Josh sitting on each side of a hospital bed.

"She's coming round," said Dad.

"She'll be all right now," added a nurse. "But it was touch and go. At one moment I thought we had lost her."

Annie's head was bandaged and she felt rather sick. "I've been a long way, over rivers and seas and mountains," she said but already the amazing journey was beginning to fade from her mind.

"We flew to the end of the universe and I had to choose whether to go on or come back to you. But Crispin wanted to return for the bending race at a gymkhana on Saturday," she said.

Mum stroked her brow. Dad fetched her some water to drink. "You fell off your bike. If only you had been wearing your helmet, you would have been all right," he said.

"You were a very silly girl, you were nearly killed," added Mum.

"I think I can ride now," said Annie dreamily. "And I may be able to read. Everything looks so different. I can read the name of the ward, it's Shelley's Ward, is that right?"

"Yes," cried Josh. "Well done."

"I know I can read small writing too and I don't hate myself any more because now I've flown around the world, I know I can do anything," said Annie.

Annie was soon home. She tried to tell people about the amazing ride she had had on Crispin but no one believed her story. But neither could anyone explain however hard they tried, how Annie had learnt so much about the world. Or why she could suddenly read; and ride better than anyone else of her age at the riding school. As for Crispin he never did arrive in time for the bending race. His owner said that he had simply vanished. "On the same day as you fell off your bike, Annie," she said. "We've searched high and low for him. We've advertised, but there's no sign of him anywhere. I just hope he isn't dog meat by now."

Annie remained silent. But she has never forgotten the ride and sometimes she imagines Crispin flying across the sky, over oceans and mountains, over countries she never knew existed until he took her there. She imagines him carrying other sick children on his warm back behind his magic wings, making them better.

So, though Annie never mentions her amazing ride, one day soon she intends

to write a book about what really
happened to her when she was lying in
a hospital bed between life and death
and how Crispin changed her life for
ever.

FLYAWAY AND THE FANTASTIC POND

Flyaway came from the riding school where Megan had learnt to ride. He was barely twelve hands high and dark brown with a dear little, white snippet on his nose. He was Megan's first pony.

Megan was eight and lived in a cottage with her parents and a dog called Treacle. A small paddock went with the cottage. It had a shelter in it, a hollow, tall trees and a pond. The cottage was called Rose Cottage and stood by itself at the end of a short country lane.

Flyaway was lonely. He had had lots of pony friends at the riding school and he missed them dreadfully. He stood at the paddock gate a lot of the time waiting for Megan. Megan thought that he was there because he loved her but actually he was waiting to be taken back to the riding school. Whenever Flyaway neighed which he did quite often, Megan rushed outside to give him a carrot or an apple.

Flyaway neighed most at night, but Megan's bedroom was at the front of the cottage so she didn't hear him, if she had she would have taken him something to eat whatever the time or the state of the weather. Flyaway knew she loved him, but she wasn't a pony; she couldn't graze beside him, or rub noses, or chew manes. And worst of all she didn't know pony language.

After a few days Megan rode Flyaway along the lane and on to a bridleway with her father walking beside her. Flyaway kept looking for the ponies from the riding school. He neighed when he saw a cow, and he stopped dead when he heard hoofs in the distance. He stared and stared, and was so excited that Megan could feel his heart beating between her legs.

"What's the matter with him?" asked Dad as they entered a wood.

"I think he's seen a ghost. Aunt Alice says that ponies can see things we can't. Maybe something terrible happened here years ago," replied Megan. "Maybe a pony was killed here by a wild animal, a dinosaur or tiger."

"I doubt it," said Dad.

Flyaway tried to be good, but he was used to going out with a crowd of ponies and it felt strange to be walking through a wood without another pony in sight. If he had been a person he might have said, "I'm lonely. I want my friends." But he couldn't, because humans don't understand pony language, which has lots of movements, but hardly any words.

Megan's father told her to sit up and use her legs. "You must be the master," he said.

They walked back through the wood. Flyaway did not want to return to his paddock. He dawdled and shied at things, which weren't there. Then he wandered into the lane just as a car was approaching. The driver hooted angrily and Dad shouted, "Sorry" and then he said, "I thought you could ride, Megan. Next time I'll bring a leading rein."

Megan sulked. She had looked forward to having Flyaway so much; now everything seemed to be going wrong. But worse was to follow, for the very next day Flyaway stopped looking over the gate for Megan. Instead he stood by the pond all day long staring into the water with pricked ears and glassy eyes. The sun was shining and if he looked hard he could see a small brown pony there with a snippet of white on his nose, and now suddenly he didn't feel lonely any more.

Sometimes when the sun went in, Flyaway saw other things in the pond,

strange shapes and fish which made ripples in the water. So gradually Flyaway began standing by the pond all day and sometimes much of the night as well. Soon he would not eat unless he was fed by the pond, not even delicious feeds full of chopped apple and sliced carrots.

Megan cried and cried. "He's not happy and he doesn't love me any more," she wailed.

"He's mad," replied Dad crossly and rang the riding school. Mrs Jones, who owned the riding school, was not pleased when Dad suggested that Flyaway was mad. She was very rude. She told Dad that it was he who needed his head examined, and that there was nothing wrong with Flyaway. Then she slammed down the telephone receiver.

"Come on, we must master Flyaway," announced Dad after a minute. "We mustn't be beaten. We'll get him away from the pond. Come on – action stations – one, two, one, two."

Dad sounded so excited that Treacle ran round and round him in circles leaping in the air and barking.

Megan fetched Flyaway's bridle. Dad found her riding whip saying, "Bribery is better than force." Mum fetched lumps of sugar from the kitchen cupboard. Treacle ran across the paddock, yapping wildly.

Flyaway was staring into the pond as usual and hardly noticed Megan putting on his bridle. When she had buckled up the throat lash, she put the reins over his head and pulled and pulled. "Walk on Flyaway, there's a good boy," she said.

Mum held the sugar under his nose. Dad waved Megan's whip. Treacle barked louder than ever. Slowly they dragged Flyaway to the gate. But when he reached it, Flyaway put down his head and galloped back to the pond, and because he went so fast, Megan let go of the reins, which became caught in his legs and broke.

"I'm certain he's mad; there's no other explanation," cried Dad.

"We had better call a vet," suggested Mum.

"Yes, maybe he's got a tumour on the

brain," replied Dad.

"What's that?" cried Megan with tears streaming down her face.

"A lump inside his head," replied Dad. "Take off his bridle, Megan and stop crying, please."

Mum hugged Megan. "Everything is going to be all right darling," she said.

Their nearest vet was called Sheila Small, who wasn't small at all, being six foot high in her socks. She listened to Flyaway's heart and to his chest. She looked down his throat with a torch. She got Mum to put a cloth over Flyaway's eyes and told Dad to lead him across the paddock; but of course, Flyaway refused to leave the pond, jibbing and rearing, so that Sheila Small said, "I see what you mean, he is a handful, the little rascal."

She tapped Flyaway's hoofs with a little hammer; then she stood back and looked at him.

"Well what's wrong?" asked Dad

impatiently.

Flyaway was looking into the pond again and nickering.

The sun had gone behind a cloud and all he could see was ripples but he knew that any minute his friend would appear again and then he wouldn't be lonely any more.

"He's mad, isn't he?" asked Dad.

"No, he's lonely. He needs a friend. That's the only explanation," replied Sheila Small.

"But he's got me," cried Megan.

"But you are not a pony. Ponies are herd animals; they live in groups, not alone. Find him a friend and if that doesn't work sell him," replied Sheila Small getting into her car.

So they found Flyaway a friend, a sad little Shetland pony who had stood all day and night, whatever the weather, tethered by his owners' house.

He was black and called Angus and his owner really didn't want him any more. Angus was lonely too. The two ponies sniffed noses and then Flyaway said, "There's a magic pond in my paddock. Come and look. It's got a little brown pony in it, not all the time, just sometimes." And he trotted away across the paddock, whinnying all the way to the pond.

Angus trotted after him. It was a very hot day and there were flies everywhere and not a cloud in the sky.

"Look there he is! Look Angus," cried Flyaway staring into the water. Angus looked into the pond and suddenly there were two ponies there. "Look, he's got a friend now, just like me," cried Flyaway beside himself with excitement.

"A friend? That's me silly," replied Angus scornfully, "And the other pony is you, stupid. It's your reflection Flyaway, like you in a mirror. Wake up, it's you, Flyaway!"

"Me? Is that what I look like," asked Flyaway, stunned by the news.

"Yes, and if you don't mind I'm going

to your nice shelter over there now. After weeks standing in the hot sun with hardly anything to eat and hardly any water, I want some shade." And Angus kicked up his heels and galloped to the shelter.

So, I've been looking at myself all these weeks, thought Flyaway, following Angus.

Then standing beside Angus in the shelter Flyaway asked, just to make sure, "So I'm the brown pony in the pond then. I'm really quite handsome, aren't I? I never knew I looked like that, and if I don't look I'm not there. Is that right, Angus?"

"Of course it's right," replied Angus. "But do stop talking, I want to sleep. It's so lovely in here with no flies to bother me. And you've got me as a friend now, Flyaway, so you don't need to stare in that pond any more."

Flyaway knew now that he had been very silly. But then he thought, if I hadn't been silly, Angus wouldn't be here and I would still be all alone. And suddenly Flyaway felt so happy that he went out of the shelter and rolled over and over in the parched summer grass.

Megan was watching over the paddock gate. "Come and look Mum," she called. "Flyaway's rolling, so I know everything is going to be all right now, because he's not standing by the pond any more."

And from then on everything was all right because now Flyaway only looked at himself occasionally in the pond just to make sure he hadn't changed. He and Angus became best friends and Flyaway became a perfect pony once more.

MINNIE AND THE
MIRACULOUS MUSHROOMS

"Minnie can manage. She's a Welsh pony and she doesn't need much food. And I'm certainly not paying someone to feed her. I haven't got that sort of money," said the rich man in the flashy car.

His children were young and believed everything he said. Their mother was more interested in her appearance than the thin dun pony standing by their paddock gate. So the Dawson family drove away for a holiday leaving Minnie alone in the wire-fenced paddock. It was October and half term was about to begin.

Minnie waited patiently for the Dawsons to return. When she had eaten every blade of grass in the paddock, she ate the leaves falling from the ash tree by the gate. She drank from the muddy pond at the end of the paddock.

Every morning at the same time, she stood staring at the large house nearby hoping that someone would appear to feed her. No one did. October became November and the ash tree was quite bare now. Minnie was very, very hungry. She would have eaten a hedge if there had been one to eat. Bits of her mane fell out and she started to itch. She rubbed her itchy bits against the gate and the ash tree, and the patches became raw and then infected.

No one ever passed Minnie's paddock, except the postman delivering letters and he was always in a hurry and not at all interested in the small dun pony starving in the paddock.

Minnie ate the bark on the ash tree. She ate the tops of the posts which held up the wire which fenced her paddock. Then one morning weak with hunger, she saw that mushrooms had suddenly appeared during the night by the pond and she ate them too. The mushrooms did not taste like anything Minnie had ever eaten before; but the more she ate the more she liked them.

And now, quite suddenly, Minnie began to feel happy which was something she hadn't felt for a long time. She lay down on the wet earth and saw her mother again and the wild, Welsh hills where she had been born. And now her paddock was changing. The ash tree was turning blue and the grass appeared orange through the mud and the sky became crimson. The strength came back into Minnie's legs and she stood up and then she galloped round and round her paddock bucking like a two-year-old.

Fortunately new mushrooms kept appearing and, as long as Minnie ate them, she was happy. At the same time without realising it, Minnie was changing. She did not grow fatter, just taller and taller so that instead of being twelve hands high she became thirteen hands and then fourteen hands. Her head grew larger too, until it became a horse's head, rather than a pony's. And her coat turned white. A neighbour called Mr Swallow delivering a letter to the house, thought that Mr Dawson must have bought himself a horse.

"He must be taking up riding," he told his wife who wondered what had happened to the little dun pony he had bought for his children.

"She was always a poor thin little thing," she said.

"Well this one isn't much better," replied Mr Swallow. "She looks like a toast rack."

"Someone should report him for cruelty," said Mrs Swallow.

But for three days the Swallows did nothing. They did not want to cause offence or upset their neighbours.

"And it's really none of our business," insisted Mr Swallow.

It was very pleasant where the Dawsons were staying, so they stayed on long past the end of half term. Then at last remembering Minnie, Mr Dawson wrote to Mr Swallow asking him to give her some hay. "She won't need much, and I'll pay you back the moment we return," he wrote.

Mr Swallow did not know a lot about ponies. But he bought a bale of hay and took some of it over to the paddock in a wheelbarrow. He did not take much, because he had forgotten that Minnie was no longer twelve hands high but had become a grey mare of fifteen two hands.

When he returned home, Mr Swallow said, "Something funny's going on. Mr Dawson told me to feed Minnie, but there's no sign of her in the paddock, just a big grey horse, bigger even than the last one I saw there."

"Perhaps she's called Minnie too," suggested Mrs Swallow with a scornful laugh.

"I don't like it. I don't like it at all," said Mr Swallow. "Would you like to come and look."

Mrs Swallow hardly ever went outside because her legs didn't work very well. She was terribly shocked when she saw Minnie.

"Can't you see the animal's starving," she shouted. "Look at the raw patches on her. Look at her eyes, they're yellow. A well horse doesn't have yellow eyes. And look at the state of her hoofs." Mrs Swallow had ridden when she was young and everything she learnt then was coming back to her. "It's disgusting," she bellowed remembering the well kept riding school ponies she had ridden. "We must ring up the RSPCA immediately."

"But we're neighbours. And supposing Mr Dawson is sent to prison," wailed Mr Swallow who admired Mr Dawson for being rich and successful.

Ignoring him, Mrs Swallow rushed home and now her legs were working quite well so that by the time she reached her back door she was almost running. Then still panting, she rang the police, the RSPCA and a local Horse Rescue Centre. "Now we'll see what happens," she said rubbing her hands together. "Let's go to the field and see who arrives first. Come on Percy." (Percy was Mr Swallow's Christian name). A policewoman arrived first and was shocked by poor Minnie's appearance. "I've never seen a horse before with yellow eyes," she said. "Is it usual?"

Mrs Swallow shook her head. "Certainly not," she said. Next a man and a woman appeared from the Horse Rescue Centre with a Land Rover and trailer and their own vet in attendance.

"That animal used to be a sandy coloured pony, but it's grown and grown and turned white. I really don't know what's going on," said Mr Swallow in a worried voice.

"Don't worry Sir. We'll handle this. You go home and stay in the warm and make yourself a nice cup of tea," the policewoman replied in a soothing voice so that Mr Swallow knew she thought he was mad.

The Horse Rescue people were too busy to listen to Mr Swallow. The vet was examining Minnie, while the other man, who was called Jim, was taking photographs of her, and the woman was patting her scrawny neck. "Will you be prosecuting Mr Dawson?" asked Mr Swallow nervously.

"Of course. This is a bad case of neglect," said the policewoman. "And it must not go unpunished. Can you give me the owner's name and address please."

"Where is her owner?" asked Jim putting away his camera.

"Abroad," replied Mr Swallow miserably. "Do you do this often?"

"Yes, all the time," said Jim.

"And who was expected to look after this unfortunate animal, while he was away," asked the policewoman, writing in a notebook.

"No one," cried Mrs Swallow. "Absolutely no one until today when my husband got a letter."

Minnie was being loaded into the trailer, when the inspector from the RSPCA arrived. She was feeling rather ill. She had eaten the last of the mushrooms two days ago and no more had appeared. And now she had the feeling that she was shrinking. The trailer was bedded with straw and there was sweet smelling hay hanging in a hay-net. The vet from the Rescue Centre had given her two injections and she was wearing a rug. The vet was extremely worried by the colour or her eyes.

Minnie was very happy at the Rescue Centre. She made friends with a forty-year-old pony called Roly; her raw patches healed and stopped itching. But she did miss the mushrooms and now she seemed to be getting smaller and smaller. The vet at the Rescue Centre was very puzzled.

"I've never seen anything like this before," he said and ordered photographs and measurements to be taken daily.

Then he called in another more famous vet who was equally perplexed. Minnie enjoyed all the attention. Soon her eyes were no longer yellow and now at last she stopped longing for mushrooms. And she actually rather liked getting smaller, preferring to be a small dun pony rather than a large grey horse.

The Dawsons returned a week later and looked for Minnie. Then Mr Dawson found a letter lying on his doormat telling him that he was to be prosecuted for cruelty to a grey mare of fifteen two hands high.

"Someone's gone crazy," he cried. "I've never owned a fifteen two hand grey horse in my life. Where's Minnie?"

The Dawson children burst into tears. They were frightened by their father's anger and they wanted Minnie back in her paddock, or thought they did.

Their mother stood looking at her face in the hall mirror. "I do believe my tan is fading already," she said.

Mr Dawson visited the Swallows and there was a terrible row.

"You reported me for being cruel to a grey horse, didn't you?" demanded Mr Dawson in a loud voice.

"Minnie's changed. It's not our fault she grew and grew," cried Mr Swallow.

"You should have made proper arrangements for your pony," stormed Mrs Swallow. "You can't just go away and leave an animal to fend for itself. Your pony or horse, whichever you like to call it, has been taken to a Horse Rescue Centre and it wasn't our doing. We were just doing our best for the poor animal."

"Well, I think you are both mad,"

shouted Mr Dawson walking out of their house and slamming the door after him. "Come on children get into the car. We're going to the Rescue Centre."

Mr Dawson drove far too fast to the Centre and was caught in a speed trap, which did not improve his temper.

When he eventually arrived there, he left his children in the car while be banged on a door marked 'office'. When a small woman in riding clothes appeared he shouted rudely, "The name is Dawson. Where is this grey horse which is supposed to belong to me?"

The woman, who was called Susan, led the way across the yard. "I'm afraid she isn't grey any more; she's back to her normal size; it's a great mystery, Mr Dawson," she said. And there was Minnie gazing over a stable door, her eyes sparkling with happiness.

"She's still very thin," continued Susan. "And why she grew and grew and turned white, no one can explain.

It is a complete mystery. She will be on TV in a few day's time; ITV have made a programme about her transformation and lots of important people are taking part."

"And who gets the money?" asked Mr Dawson.

"What money?" asked Susan, patting Minnie.

"The money for the programme," replied Mr Dawson.

"I don't think there's any money involved. Vets are still doing tests. Her eyes were quite yellow when she came here," explained Susan.

"Well, I want her back. She must be worth a fortune now," said Mr Dawson.

"I believe there's a court case coming up," replied Susan. "And Minnie stays here until it's settled and when people see her on TV, still looking so thin and hear her story I think you're going to get a lot of hate mail, Mr Dawson."

Mr Dawson drove home in an even

worse temper than before.

As for Minnie, to this day, no one has discovered why she grew so tall and changed into a horse and then changed back again.

She did appear on TV and became a celebrity. Mr Dawson was not allowed to have her back. The Rescue Centre kept her until she was well again and then found her a lovely home where she is greatly loved.

But the mystery remains. The mushrooms have never appeared again in the Dawsons' paddock and no horse has eaten the same kind before or since and Minnie cannot tell anyone what she ate, being only a pony. So really, just you and I know the real story. Mr Dawson has been banned from keeping a pony ever again. Luckily his children didn't really mind because his daughter likes being clean and tidy and you can't be that if you are looking after a pony. And the two boys have always been more interested in trains than a small dun pony that needed feeding every day whatever the weather.

Finally if you see strange mushrooms suddenly appearing, DON'T eat them; they may be poisonous and can kill you. Minnie just happened to be lucky.

CARLOTTA'S DREAM

Mrs Hardy and Lauren drove into our yard in a Land Rover with trailer attached. I was picking out Biscuit, our donkey's, hoofs. He's very old and very wise.

"Oh Carlotta, can you help? You're our last hope?" cried Mrs Hardy, leaping out of the Land Rover (I am called Carlotta after my Italian Grandmother). "We've been invited to my youngest sister's wedding in Spain and Lauren is chief bridesmaid and it's the day after tomorrow. We've been let down at the last minute by Jean Metcalf who should have been looking after Brandy. Can you possibly help out? He won't be any trouble."

Lauren who was a little older than I am, was already unboxing chestnut

Brandy. "You can put him in your paddock during the day and in the stable at night," continued Mrs Hardy.

"We'll bring you back something really great from Spain," promised Lauren smiling at me.

Dad appeared then. "Oh, hello there," cried Mrs Hardy and explained their problem all over again. "Oh goodness, we must go," she finished. "Just look at the time and we've got a plane to catch. We'll bring you back litres of super wine," she said peering up at Dad, who is a lanky six footer with a mop of wild, red brown hair on his head.

"We haven't got any hay," said Dad.

"We've brought two bales. We'll be back on Sunday night and if there's any left you can keep it for your old donkey," replied Mrs Hardy.

The Hardys had bedded down our best loose box with straw, filled up five hay-nets for Brandy and filled up two buckets of water all at the speed of an express train. They seemed to have thought of everything except that we might have said 'no'. They had left a bag of hard feed in our tiny tack room with a list of directions on it. Then they had gone.

Mum was furious when she saw what had happened.

"We hardly know them and they do this to us," she complained.

"I'll look after Brandy. It will be good practice for when I have a pony of my own," I said.

"But you're only nine," replied Mum.

The Hardys hadn't left any tack for Brandy, just a cheap nylon head-collar with a rope attached.

But even if they had, I wouldn't have ridden him – I'm just not good enough. Biscuit was looking over the fence and brayed several times.

"At least someone's pleased," said Dad.

"When does the pony go?" asked Mum, still angry.

"Well the wedding's the day after tomorrow, so I suppose they'll be back on Sunday, that's what they said," replied Dad.

"Did they leave an address?" asked Mum.

Dad shook his head.

"We hardly know them, and they do this to us. It's such cheek," wailed Mum. "And supposing something happens to their pony?"

"It won't," replied Dad and none of us touched wood.

Later I read the feeding instructions the Hardys had left. Brandy's feeds were really complicated with additions of powdered garlic, cod liver oil, chopped apple and grated carrot. I fed him at six o'clock and he was really pushy, unlike Biscuit who waits patiently for his feed.

I gave him his hay-net, which had a label on it saying, No 1 and filled up his water bucket. I wanted to pat him but he swung his quarters towards me and continued scoffing his feed.

Before I went to bed I set my alarm clock for seven and I thought it's really great having a pony to look after and excellent practice for when I have one of my own.

It was April and when I woke up the next morning the birds were singing outside my window and the sun was shining. Leaping from my bed I switched off my alarm clock before rushing outside in my pyjamas, only stopping to put on boots on the way. As I opened the back door, Biscuit hee-hawed desperately from our paddock. "It's all right, I'm coming," I called. "Don't worry." But I should have known it was some sort of cry for help, because Biscuit doesn't usually bray at seven o'clock in the morning.

"Hi, there," I yelled to Biscuit before turning to look at Brandy but Brandy wasn't there. His box door stood open, his hay-net was empty, and his bucket was tipped over. I took it all in without really seeing it. The next moment I was in the house again, shouting, "Brandy isn't there. He's gone. The box is empty. Do something."

At first my parents didn't believe me. "His door is wide open. He's been stolen or something," I cried.

"I'll ring the Hardys. Their number must be in the book, they may not have left yet," said Mum.

Pulling on some trousers, Dad followed me outside. "You're right, he has gone," he said. "But there are no fresh tyre marks, so nothing to go on," he added looking at the gravel.

"If we had a dog, he or she would have raised the alarm," I said disagreeably. "Why can't we have a dog." And now I was crying, already imagining the Hardys' return, and their anger.

Dad returned indoors. Mum rang the police before we set out on our bikes to look for Brandy. We went to his home first, which was three miles away and was called the Cedars. But there was only a cat mewing pathetically by the front door. As we turned our bikes round, Mum said, "Are you sure you locked his stable door properly yesterday evening, Carlotta?"

"Yes," I shouted but even as I answered, I couldn't remember actually doing it. If I had, it had been automatic, like washing your hands without thinking or pulling on your socks, or switching on a kettle. And now I thought, if Brandy's killed, no one will ever forgive me.

I would rather forget the rest of that day. Mum and Dad rang everyone they knew who might be able to help. They rang the police again. Finally they rang the Frasers whom everyone knows are the Hardys' best friends. Mrs Fraser answered and she sounded just like Mrs Hardy (I was listening on our phone upstairs). "Brandy's probably dog's meat by now. You had better start ringing all the abattoirs. He was freeze marked, but I can't tell you his number," she said. "Don't you keep your yard gate padlocked. He's a valuable pony and Lauren will never get over losing him, never ever. One doesn't, not if one loves an animal. It's worse than losing a friend," she said. I didn't listen to any more. Suddenly I wanted to die.

"No help there," said Mum a moment later. "Come on darling, into bed with you. You look half-dead. We'll find him, never fear. Don't give up."

"But tomorrow's Saturday and they'll be here again on Sunday for sure, and supposing he's still missing?"

"It's their fault. We didn't ask for him to be plonked on us, and you're too young to be responsible for a valuable pony," replied Mum.

But it didn't seem like that to me. I lay in bed imagining returning to school.

Lauren is in a higher class and she would tell everyone what had happened. They would look at me and say, "Why didn't you bolt the stable door, stupid?" And I wouldn't have an answer. So lying in bed I prayed, "Oh God, please let Brandy be found before the Hardys' return. Please, please." But I didn't think God would listen, because only a little bit of me believes in him and I never go to church.

At ten o'clock Mum and Dad went to bed. The telephone hadn't rung all evening. Mum peeped round the corner of my door. "Go to sleep, darling. Stop worrying; everything will turn out all right in the end," she said.

But it was a long time before I slept. And when I did, I was pursued by the Hardys in my dreams screaming at me, "It's all your fault, Carlotta. Why didn't you bolt the stable door."

And then quite suddenly the dream changed and now it seemed absolutely real. I was walking down a long tree lined drive which led to a lawn and a large house with pillars by an impressive front door and all the time I was calling "Brandy, where are you?"

There was a moon in the sky riding high between wild grey clouds. And a great silence. And then I heard a whinny quite near and I was running and shouting, "Brandy where are you. Come on, there's a good boy." And now I saw a swimming pool with its cover half off and Brandy standing in a few inches of water, but even as I saw him, I woke up. It was still dark outside. I remember thinking, if only it could be true, if only it wasn't just a dream, 'if only, if only', and I knew now why Mum calls those two words the saddest words in the English language. I slept again a brief dreamless sleep and woke and saw the swimming pool again. If only it could be true, I thought going down to a breakfast I didn't want.

"You were shouting in your sleep, "Brandy where are you?" said Mum drinking coffee.

"Do dreams come true because if they do, I think I've found him," I said. "He's in a swimming pool by a big house with pillars and a long drive up to it."

Mum looked at Dad. Dad looked at Mum and then one of them said, "Spindle Park. It's not far and it's got a long drive. Come on, let's go."

We forgot all about our breakfast. We leapt into the car. It wasn't far to Spindle Park, the whole place had a wonderful brick and flint wall round it and there were notices everywhere saying KEEP OUT and PRIVATE PROPERTY. Otherwise it was the same as in my dream. And Brandy *was* in the swimming pool just as I had dreamt. He gave a loud neigh when he saw us.

"Stupid animal. He must have fallen in," said Dad.

"But how are we going to get him out?"

asked Mum.

The pool was half covered by a plastic sheet. "I could get into it," I suggested.

"But he can't get out. He's got to be lifted out," replied Mum. "And I don't want you falling under the cover and getting drowned."

"The fire brigade. We need the fire brigade," announced Dad running towards the house. I ran after him. Together we pulled the bell by the front door, and waited. And my heart was beating wildly, full of hope. It took a long time for anyone to open the door, but at last, an elderly man stood staring at us as though we had just appeared from outer space. "His Lordship is abroad," said the old man beginning to close the door again.

"There's a pony in the swimming pool. We need the fire brigade," said Dad. The door was on the chain now. "I'll ring them," said the old man. "I'm taking your word for it. If it's a hoax you'll pay for it."

We returned to the swimming pool and waited. "He thought we were thieves, didn't he?" I asked.

"When old people are on their own they're always afraid," said Dad. "I expect there are valuables inside which he didn't want us to see – pictures, silver, antiques."

"So dreams do come true," I said.

A fire engine appeared quite soon without its sirens blaring. "Where's the pony then," asked the tallest fire fighter. "Come on lads, who wants to get their feet wet."

Two men jumped into the pool and put what they called struts round Brandy, which were really wide straps. They were attached to a small crane on the fire engine and five minutes later Brandy was standing on dry land again. I put on his head-collar and a fire fighter pressed a button on the fire engine and the struts fell off. It was magical.

Then Mum and I set off for home with Brandy while Dad thanked the fire fighters. "There's something to pay, but I've told them to send the bill to the Hardys," he called as he passed us in the car.

"But it was my fault," I yelled.

"We can't pay. We haven't got the money, and we didn't want their pony; at least I didn't," cried Mum.

Brandy threw his head around, and pulled and wouldn't walk. By the time we reached home again our arms were aching.

"We'll padlock his door this time," Dad said.

I was glad Brandy hadn't been stolen as I dried his legs with straw. I gave him a feed and hay and filled up his bucket of water again. Then we had lunch - ham, salad and new potatoes and ice cream.

"I expect the Hardys are feasting, Mum," I said.

"I expect they're drunk," replied Dad.

"What are we going to tell them?" I asked.

"Nothing," replied Dad.

"But you rang up all those people – everyone knows," I said.

"And then there will be the bill from

the fire fighters. We'll have to tell them it was all my fault, because I didn't bolt his door properly. We can't lie," I said.

At nine o'clock that night, just as I was going to bed, we heard a Land Rover drive into our yard and then there was a banging on the back door loud enough to shake the house.

Mum opened it. "Where is Brandy? Have you found him?" shouted Mrs Hardy. "What happened? You know we paid five thousand pounds for him."

Lauren was standing behind her, with a face wet with tears.

"He's in the stable. He's all right," I said.

"We've come back early. The Frasers rang us," said Mrs Hardy. "Apparently the whole of the Pony Club are looking for him."

"He's over here," I said, leading the way to the stable.

The Hardys had forgotten the presents they had promised. They came indoors and drank coffee. Mum and Dad told them the whole story. "I can't have bolted the door properly. I was so excited at having a pony to look after that I must have forgotten," I confessed.

Then Mrs Hardy and Lauren looked at each other before Mrs Hardy replied, "No it wasn't your fault, Carlotta. It was ours. We should have told you that Brandy is an expert at unbolting doors. We have three bolts on his door at home."

"And I think I know why he went to Spindle Park, because we had Pony Club Camp there last year," said Lauren.

I didn't tell them about my dream and gradually my feeling of guilt ebbed away, but I couldn't stop thinking, supposing I hadn't had the dream, how long would Brandy have stood in the swimming pool, undiscovered? Would the old man have found him eventually? Or would he have died there?

Mrs Hardy kissed me when she left. "We'll fetch Brandy tomorrow and we haven't forgotten we promised you a present, Carlotta," she said. "And remember we'll do anything for you any time, don't forget to ask."

When they had gone, I sat on a chair in the kitchen and cried with relief, mostly because Brandy's escape hadn't been my fault after all; while Dad said, "I hope you'll have more dreams soon, Carlotta. You might dream which horse wins the Derby, or better still, The National Lottery numbers, then we'll be really rich and you can have half a dozen ponies. But I didn't want half a dozen ponies. I just wanted my dream one – a roan pony with a silver coloured mane, a mare who wasn't pushy and couldn't open doors and that really would be a dream come true.

SNOWDROP AND
THE MAGIC BIRD

Snowdrop was an old nearly white Welsh pony. She belonged to Penny who was nine years old and loved him more than anything else in the world.

Snowdrop was half-asleep in her stable when the magic bird flew in and woke her up. The bird was very beautiful. He was the size of an eagle with a beak like a blackbird and his purply wings were tipped with gold. He wasn't only beautiful, he was clever, too. Perching on a beam the magic bird looked at Snowdrop with eyes which shone like little lamps in the dusk, and said, "You're Snowdrop and you are twenty five years old and you've been having trouble with your teeth. Is that correct?"

Snowdrop was wide awake now. "How do you know about my teeth," she asked. "And my age; and how come you can speak pony language so well?"

"Now listen to me, Snowdrop," said the bird in a slightly croaky voice. "What do you want most in all the world?"

But Snowdrop only replied, "How do you know about my teeth. No one else does. I wish they did."

"The robin told me, the one who sits on your manger every morning sharing your breakfast. Now tell me what you want me to do. I am an exceedingly busy bird and can't stay here talking."

Snowdrop looked around her comfortable loose box. She looked at the net full of sweet smelling hay hanging in one corner and at the bucket half full of clean water in another and she couldn't think of anything she really wanted.

"Hurry up," said the magic bird. "I have

two more visits to make this evening and it's almost dark already.

Snowdrop thought and thought and at last she said, "I would like to speak to Penny in her own language; but that's impossible, isn't it?"

"Nothing is impossible. I know a hundred languages. I even know mole language," replied the bird proudly.

"If I neigh now Penny will come running. She worries about me all day long," said Snowdrop suddenly excited. And then Snowdrop gave a very long, very loud neigh, which left her all puffed out.

The magic bird wore a very pretty expensive looking watch on his right leg just above his rather long claws. He looked at it now and said, "You can only have one hundred seconds. No more and no less. Do you understand?"

"But I can't tell the time," cried Snowdrop.

"I'll do it for you. Just say to me what you want to say and I'll flap my wings once when you are reaching the time and twice when your time is up. And don't forget to mention your teeth," instructed the magic bird.

Penny was having tea with her parents when Snowdrop neighed. She was eating a particularly delicious little cake, which she immediately stopped eating.

"Oh dear, what can have happened. I'll go and have a look I won't be a moment," she cried before she put on her wellies and rushed outside.

"She's coming. What shall I say?" cried Snowdrop anxiously.

"Just think and I will say it in English, Snowdrop. Stop worrying," replied the magic bird. "Stay calm. I won't be able to understand you if you are all wound up."

Snowdrop looked at Penny who was looking pretty and worried at the same time and her thoughts came out like this:

"Hello, Penny. I love you but there are one or two things I must mention while I can talk to you which won't be for long:

Number 1 - I need a horse dentist to look at my teeth. I don't leave my breakfast because I don't like it. I can never eat it all because my teeth ache all the time.

Number 2 - I would like to have a friend. I'm lonely living by myself.

Number 3 - My shoes hurt my hoofs. Can you have them removed or buy me a new set please?

Number 4 - I don't like my kimblewick bit, I'd like a plain jointed snaffle which I can jingle in my mouth.

Number 5 - I came from Welsh Mountains and unless it's really cold, I'd like to live outside where I can see the stars shining in the night sky.

Number 6 - I grow older and you grow heavier. Can I retire soon please."

Then Snowdrop looked at the magic bird and he flapped his wings once and said in pony language, which is a strange quiet language, "You can say a little more. Think of a few appropriate words."

So Snowdrop said, "One day I would like to go to the sea, because I've never seen it properly but most of all I want a friend."

The magic bird flapped his wings twice and then Snowdrop knew she had used up all her time. She went away and stood at the back of her stable feeling very odd and waited for Penny to say something. For a moment Penny was transfixed. Then she cried, "Go on please, go on," and when Snowdrop stayed silent she rushed outside calling, "Mum, Dad come quickly. Snowdrop can talk."

And at that very moment the magic bird flapped his gold tipped wings and flew over Penny's head into the night sky, his eyes shining like little lamps in the darkness which had suddenly fallen.

Penny's parents arrived, panting and all agog.

"Let's hear her talk," they cried and then as Snowdrop stayed silent, her father said, "You've invented it or imagined it. She can't speak at all."

"A big bird flew out over our heads. Did you see it?" asked her mother. And it was then that Penny decided that the bird had done the talking, not Snowdrop; but all the same, she said in a hopeless voice, "Speak Snowdrop. Please speak."

But Snowdrop could not think of anything more she wanted to say and now the bird had gone she knew she couldn't speak anyway. So to calm her nerves she started nibbling at the hay in her hay-net.

"I think it was something to do with the bird. I think it did the talking. It was really, really scary. Poor Snowdrop said that I was getting too heavy for her, and that she needs her teeth looked at by a horse dentist, and she wants a friend," said Penny beginning to cry.

"What utter rubbish," cried her father who was a computer expert and liked things to be logical and clear cut and didn't believe in magic.

"And she wants to wear a snaffle bit and go to the sea. And I thought I was a good home," cried Penny crying louder than ever.

"I feel such a failure. I thought she was really happy here; but she isn't," she wailed.

Then Snowdrop put her head on Penny's shoulder and blew lovely pony breath which is sweeter than the most expensive perfume over her face. And now Snowdrop wanted to say something like: "None of it is that important, so please don't cry." But of course she couldn't because the magic bird had flown away and Penny couldn't understand pony language.

Penny's father put his arms around her, because he couldn't bear to see her cry, and he said, "We'll get you a bigger pony and that's a promise." And her mother added, "And we will get a horse dentist as soon as we can find one to deal with Snowdrop's teeth. No wonder she kept leaving her breakfast if they're hurting."

"But don't tell people about the bird and Snowdrop talking because there's no such thing as magic and they'll only think you're crazy," said Penny's father.

"But she did talk, and you did see the magic bird, didn't you, Mum?" asked Penny.

"Yes, we did see a very strange bird," agreed her mother.

"But not a magic one," insisted Penny's father. "It was probably one that escaped from a zoo."

So after hugging Snowdrop, Penny went indoors and finished the delicious little cake she had been eating when Snowdrop neighed so loudly.

Penny did not tell her friends about the magic bird until a small piece appeared in the local paper entitled A STRANGE BIRD PERFORMS MIRACLES. It told how an extraordinary bird had flown into a farmyard and somehow released a dog from a shed where it had been hidden away and half starved for many months. And then how the same bird had been seen again in the sky minutes before a sow had somehow escaped from the tethers which tied her to her sty floor. Neither animal had been seen again, though it was believed that the sow was living happily in a nearby forest with another pig, which had escaped from an abattoir.

But few of Penny's friends believed her story, they said things like: "You're just making it up," and "You know it isn't true because we all know ponies don't talk."

But Penny didn't really mind, because whatever they said she knew it was true. Her parents soon found a friend for Snowdrop, a five year old called Sailor who was rather plain with a black head and a mainly white body. He was also very well behaved.

Snowdrop's shoes were taken off and never put on again. And now when Penny rides her, which isn't often because she has Sailor to ride, she rides her in a snaffle bit, which Snowdrop can jingle between her teeth, because best of all the horse dentist has been. After saying that Snowdrop's teeth were the worst he had ever seen, he has rasped them with a long rasp which has improved them no end.

Snowdrop is still waiting to see the sea. And often she longs for the magic bird to return so that she can thank him for all he has done for her.

But he's far too busy releasing hens from battery cages and dogs from terrible circumstances, and starving cats from dark sheds and horses tethered on chains in blinding heat or freezing blizzards to call again on a little old pony with a wonderful home.

Snowdrop has never forgotten what he did for her, and though she can now gobble up her feeds without pain, she always leaves a bit for the little robin, who, by contacting the magic bird, changed her life for ever.